You, Me and the Butterfly

Ready to 'fly again'

Simeon Sturney

Set in a women's prison, this is a story of fear,
hope and breakthrough.

First Published 2024 by Grace and Down Publishing,
an imprint of Malcolm Down Publishing Limited.

www.malcolmdown.co.uk

28 27 26 25 24   7 6 5 4 3 2 1

British Library Cataloguing in Publication Data
A catalogue record for this book is available from
the British Library.

ISBN 978-1-915046-88-8

Cover design by Angela Selfe

Art direction by Sarah Grace

Designed and Typeset by 2K/DENMARK
using Grace Typeface.

The Grace Typeface is designed for inclusive reading
and has been developed by 2K/DENMARK.

Printed in the UK

I have dedicated *You, Me and the Butterfly* to all those people ready to 'fly' and those who are unsure if they can ever 'go again'! I have journeyed with some amazing people, some of whom still struggle, while others have overcome huge challenges in their lives. It has been a privilege to walk alongside so many people at the lowest point in their lives. Thank you for allowing me to be a part of your story – I'm pleased you are a part of mine.

Simeon Sturney

Contents

Butterfly Drawings: There are three line drawings of a butterfly throughout the book. You are invited to colour them in if you wish. You may choose to colour in according to how you are feeling at the time.

Preface

You, Me and the Butterfly takes place in a women's prison, where failure, depression, anxiety and fear are never far away. Success, joy, peace and hope seem an unreachable dream at times. This is where we find 'You' – in prison with little hope of a positive release from the cycle which engulfs her.

Can she see change in her circumstances and environment? Can she dare for a better tomorrow, next week or next month? Looking beyond today appears pointless. 'Me' is someone trying to support 'You', when given the chance and the right resources. Yet there could be hope. Can a 'Butterfly' provide the inspiration and motivation to prompt change?

This is not just a story about someone in prison, but one to encourage anyone feeling stuck in their circumstances, unable to move on or see a brighter tomorrow.

Part One: The Story

Chapter One: You

It's another day in the women's prison you know all too well. It's just like the day before and the one before that – 'same s**t, different day' – as the saying goes. Except this day is slightly different because you're in countdown mode. Your release, 'on the out', is getting noticeably closer.

You've been in prison a little while, it may be your ninth or tenth stretch, and you've stopped counting even if others haven't. You've been there so often you know the daily routine, the pace of life and where everything is. You know when to smile or cry, and when to look strong or vulnerable. You save the vulnerable look for the officers, the tears for the chaplain, but for the other prisoners, you maintain a strong smile. You never show the scared or frightened look – not to anyone. Not ever.

Right now, you're wearing the 'hard woman' look – the one that says, 'Don't' mess with me' or 'I'm not interested, so go away.' Your face is deliberately blank, disengaged and disinterested. Officers know when to bother you and when to leave you alone. You know most of them on your wing, although there are always a few newbies you've not come across before. You can always tell a new officer by how keen they appear – so ready to help and some can be easily taken advantage of.

Of course, some officers are power crazy and love swinging their keys, barking orders and having their favourite prisoners, but you know there are some good ones as well, who listen and tell you exactly how 'it' is.

They do this in a nice way but with honesty and authority, and if they say they'll do something, they do it and if they can't, they'll tell you. Every prisoner likes to know 'where they stand' and have clarity because after all, false promises are aggravating.

The prison has been around some while but doesn't smell like some can, other than when the onsite sanitation tank is emptied. You hate the awful, overpowering stink of poo that fills the air. Thankfully, that only happens once a fortnight and is not close to the house blocks. Bad as the smell is, it's not as impacting as the noise of the prisoners you encounter when you first go onto the house block.

The smell of poo is on the other side of the prison, but the noise is all around you. It hits you every time, especially when you've been away from prison for a while, or if you arrive at medication time (when the meds are being dispensed). Yet you fairly quickly get used to it. Some prisoners even miss the noise when they leave, just like the rattling of the keys – a familiar sound to every prisoner.

Your thoughts are now turning to leaving this familiar place. This time you've been in for a couple of months and the magistrates are beginning to get fed up with you. It used to be only a few weeks for shoplifting, but now they're getting tougher the more they see you. Once, you got convicted of common assault for violence – you got four months, you hit a store security guard when they tried to stop you leaving with a leather jacket.

You've been in and out over the past ten years. You haven't come in every year, but some years, you've come back a couple of times. This has been the case recently; these days you don't run like you used to and prison is a risk you take for the lifestyle you lead, 'in and out' is part of life.

People are starting to talk about you getting out now and what happens next. You know what's coming. Some prisoners, when they know someone is going, can start to angle for favours. They'll soon be asking for your belongings or things they want you to do for them when you're out. Prison officers can start to wind you up about how long you'll last outside. You were invited to a meeting to discuss your release plans. 'Invited' sounds a bit posh, the reality is you were told you were having a meeting.

In fact, it wasn't really a meeting after all, as the only people there were you and your caseworker from inside the prison, but you didn't know that until you turned up. The Offender Manager from Probation outside couldn't make it; the wing officer who was due to be there has been pulled to cover somewhere else; the Recovery worker had taken leave at short notice, and someone from Housing wasn't there either.

So, it turned into a chat – again. If it had been your first time inside, you would have been disappointed as you may have been hopeful some of your fears would have been addressed. But it isn't and there you are again, counting down the days to nowhere.

Since the drugs got a hold of you, life has changed, but it is what it is. You tell yourself the drugs are the medicine you need. No one understands how you feel, no one 'gets it'. You've got to be an addict to know how it helps or at least been there at some point in your life. You know your family don't get it and didn't get it. The truth is, you blame them for some of the crap that has come your way and almost all of it, you don't want to talk about. It's too painful, too real. Anyway, most of the family are out of your life now, so it's just Nan who keeps in touch when you're inside and sends money in when she can. That is, of course, only when you let her know where you are. You've got friends on the street, but they are in the same situation as you. You've had a few boyfriends, although some have seemed more like punters.

You've had a couple of boyfriends who have smacked you around a bit and wanted to control you by knowing your every move and often ringing you every hour to check in. You knew if they didn't believe you, then you were in for trouble when you got back. Working the street and shoplifting, with a little bit of card fraud, is the way to get the 'gear' when there's no one around doing you a 'favour', and 'favours' usually cost.

Nan's money is small compared to what you can earn outside, and it takes a day or so to let people know you're back. Her money may be small, but you know it costs her big – as it comes out of her pension. This is one favour that doesn't come with the normal strings attached.

You've been out before and relied on 'favours', somewhere to sleep for a few nights but that comes with some form of payment: sexual favours, dealing or running drugs, or nicking 'to order'. There's no tenancy agreement signed here, the only thing you sign up to is the risk you take. You might be battered, raped or pimped, but at least you've got a roof over your head, and you know the rules. There are no rules.

You tell yourself you're a free agent, that you make up the rules and no one is going to tell you what to do. Except you know that's not exactly true. Again, you tell yourself that you are only going by 'their' rules cos you want something from them and

you're 'using' them. Everybody 'uses' everybody
on the street, so that's fair – it's the way it is.

You didn't choose this life, it chose you. Stuff in the past
wasn't good, but you're not thinking about that. What's
the point? You talked to someone once and here you are.
Some say you got in with the wrong crowd, but maybe
they were the only crowd around. Maybe you made some
bad choices, but maybe you didn't think you had choices.

Some say you deserve what you get – 'you've made
your bed, now lie in it', even though you don't own
a bed. In fact, you don't own much. You've got some
bits with a mate and a charity has some things
they said they'd look after. It's been months or
maybe longer since you talked to them, so they may
have got rid of your belongings. You hope not.

The other prisoners on the landing are starting to talk
about when you're getting out again. One woman offers
to ask her boyfriend to look out for you. Another wants
you to leave some money from your discharge grant
for her. A couple of women ask for your trainers while
suggesting you can leave wearing your prison issue
sliders. Plus they want your coat, which you don't have
anymore, and some smelly stuff you nicked from another
girl before you changed wings. But now you've promised
the same stuff to different women. It feels like everyone
wants something from you and it's doing your head in.

There's a young woman, Sammy, who you've been looking
out for. She's vulnerable, younger than you, and it's
her first time in. You'd like to leave her something, but
you know it would be taken off her or she'd trade it for
something else once you've gone. And then there's the
money you owe for the 'smoke' you had a few weeks ago.

That needs to be sorted. Even though, officially, there is nothing to smoke inside, just a vape and no lighter, but still there's 'weed' and 'a spark' if you know where to look. And you are resourceful. The prisoners don't mean to be hard on each other but on the road, you look out for yourself and it's no different inside. Even though the women tell each other they've got each other's backs, they can easily forget; you know it happens all the time. Anyway, it's simpler to keep on making promises than to explain why you're not going to give them the trainers or put money in an envelope for them or write.

You'd like to keep in touch with Sammy, but you know that could complicate things. You don't want to be tied to writing to her or giving her your 'real' phone number (not the fake one you give all the other prisoners). Even though you get on OK, you don't want to risk her passing the number on to others or her ringing you all the time with her problems, wanting money or 'gear' when she's out, or even a place to stay in an emergency. 'It'll be just for a couple of nights,' you can hear her say.

But you know it could easily turn into a couple of weeks, and not just her but her mates who need somewhere to crash, and before you know it, you could be 'cuckooed'. She's young – nineteen years old – and maybe a first timer but she's 'streetwise' and that makes you wary. Inside, she appears a little naïve, but she's pretty sharp and quick to learn. Sadly, the drugs have already started to have an effect. She's been smoking weed since she was twelve and she can be a little paranoid at times, thinking everyone is talking about her.

She talks a lot about her boyfriend, who is nearly twenty years older than her, and people do talk about that. You've been there too. Having had the older man as a boyfriend or 'sugar daddy' who paid for everything, until he wanted to do things with you and other men, things you really didn't want to do. You had to get out quickly, before things got nasty. But Sammy is in the early stages of this 'perfect' relationship. He pays for her to be pampered every week.

Although her blonde hair-dye is now fading and her nails are broken, you can see someone has been looking after her. You want to warn her that it's not going to end well, but you know she's not ready to listen, and neither were you thirteen years ago. It's been a long time since you've had an expensive haircut or worn the latest fashion – even though you've nicked it but you hardly ever get to wear it; it's usually nicked to order or you know someone who would love it.

These days you wear things that don't draw attention to yourself and keep your hair at shoulder length with its natural mousey-brown colour. The only thing noticeable about you is how skinny you are. That's what drug use and not eating does to you. Inside, you put on a little weight, but you don't like looking in the mirror. There are some prisoners who are always looking at themselves.

When inside, it's easy to become self-absorbed. It is as if the world revolves around you. What you eat, who you talk to, what 'work' or activity you do, how well you are engaging with the system and how you're feeling. You have listened to Sammy talk a lot about herself. You've told her that when you leave, she could go to the Safer Custody team and have a chat if she's feeling low. Or she could go to Chaplaincy because they are good at listening. Her immediate response was, 'I ain't religious, I don't need God.'

'Tell them you need to light a candle for your nan. That will get you off the wing and then you can

have a chat. They don't all talk about God, some
are good at just listening and if you're feeling
bad, it's a nice place to go,' you tell her.

'Why do I want to light a candle for my nan? She ain't
dead.' Sammy wasn't convinced this was a good idea.

'Nor was mine – they didn't know she wasn't dead.
I lit a candle and had a chat. They even made me
a real cup of coffee.' You smile. 'One chaplain still
asks me if I go to my nan's grave when I'm out.'

'Do you?' Sammy asks.

You frown. 'I've just told you; she isn't dead.'

'So why did you tell them that?' Sammy wasn't getting it.

'Cos I wanted a chat and a coffee,' you say with your
arms open wide and your head slightly tilted to one side.
Sammy's not always as smart as you think. Anyway, you
haven't got the time or energy to worry about Sammy
right now, you've got other things on your mind.

Back to the meeting, and there you are again, talking to
someone inside who knows they're telling you what you
already know. Your caseworker went over the same stuff:
'Turn up to your probation appointments; go to Housing
and they will have temporary accommodation; don't go to
where you are banned from, and make sure you take your
correct medication.'

You know they know you are not going to do any of it, but
you nodded and they smiled – that's the way it works. You
both walked away thinking, 'That was a waste of time.' You
were particularly annoyed as you had made an effort for

this meeting, washing your hair and putting on your nicest T-shirt, thinking there would be others there to impress. 'Why bother?' comes to mind again.

Once back on the wing, you start to make phone calls to begin Plan B, which is the usual plan that works, to a point. You call a mate who you know will 'look after you' for a night or two, with the usual payment. You don't like the plan, but what choice do you have? You know that for you to cope with Plan B, the moment you get out you'll need a few stiff drinks, just to take the edge off what's coming next. You also ring your dealer with details of the plan.

These days, you can end up doing the things your 'sugar daddy' wanted you to do all those years ago, but you tell yourself that it's your choice, and you say when, where and how much. Sadly, the need for money is greater on some occasions and you find yourself cutting your prices and being less fussed about the hygiene and location of where the transaction takes place than you would like to be.

Sometimes there's a lot of competition for the services you offer and now you're over thirty, you aren't always first pick. So, that's why you have to offer something different, even if it's at a low price, in order to earn what you need. Anyway, you've made the calls, and everything is set up for your release.

Your release plan is to walk out the gate alone, down a few cans of cider (paid for with your release grant), then get a train with the train warrant the prison will give you, and finally hop on a bus to your 'dealer's' place, paying for the drugs from the remainder of your grant. Then you'll turn up at your friend's pad with some drugs and, later that night, go out and earn some more money to keep each day ticking on the same way as before.

Chapter Two: Me

Well, here I am. You know me. You've known me for quite a while, as I'm a member of staff. You and me, we've got on OK over the months, or has it been years? It seems like years. Sometimes, you barely tolerate me, almost blanking me when we pass each other around the building. At other times, you engage well. Maybe there has been a harsh word exchanged in the past, but we move on quickly. Although I've known you to hold grudges against others, you don't with me, thankfully.

'You're alright you are,' you've said to me
on a few occasions.

'Only "alright"?' I joke back and shake my head.

'We can all improve,' you retort, forgetting that
you say it every time.

In the spirit of banter, I reply, 'And when are you
going to improve?'

Normally, you reply by giving me the one finger gesture, and that often brings our dialogue to a close. I often walk away wondering if I've made a difference. Sometimes I ask myself, 'Who am I, what can I do?'

As you know, I try to be the one who co-ordinates your case while you're here in prison. As your caseworker, I've written a few reports on you and read a few about you, even the one about a fight you had that didn't make for good reading. No one really knows what happened or why you saw 'red'. I remember you were vague about it, something to do with the portions of food you were given by the servery worker. I was there. I had just come to see you when it all kicked off. You lost it big time and ended up in the block – not your finest hour. The prisoner needed to be checked out, but thankfully she was alright.

I say it's me who tries to co-ordinate things, but it isn't easy at times. You don't make it easy, not turning up for appointments, not engaging in conversation and getting into the occasional fight. I know you complain when people don't turn up when they say they are going to, but you're the worst. I've phoned the house block when you've been a 'no show' and they've told me you don't feel well or haven't returned from work as they asked you to.

As you know, I often struggle to get everybody together to discuss how we can support you, or at least get input from the different departments. Chasing them up can be hard work. And when the reports or meetings don't match up as they should, it's me who gets into trouble. But that is all part of the job and we do it because we want to make a difference.

I say 'we' as there are many people just like me who have worked with you and would say, 'What about me – I've supported you too?'

There's 'me' the wing officer, who has known you for a while and listened when things haven't gone well for you. Who, when it was your first time in prison, took the time to explain how things work on the 'wing' and has put up with your complaining and frustrations, as well as contacting a few departments to get you more support. Often, all this without a 'thank you'. In fact, there have been several prison officers who have given you time and space over the months and years when you've been inside – some of them sticking their necks out for you.

The 'me' from Safer Custody – the team who supported you when you were feeling very low after you heard the news that your friend from outside had died. And the 'me' from Chaplaincy who arranged for you to light a candle as you reflected upon your friend's life, as well as the 'me' who was a nurse and who made sure you got medication at that time. That was a difficult time for you as you were very close to that friend, they even visited you once in prison. We know it was hard for you not to be allowed to attend the funeral, as you weren't close family, even though they were one of the closest people in your life.

And of course, there's the 'me', the art tutor who entered your work into the national competition, as well as arranging for you to have extra support in education for your reading, which has really come on now. And the 'me' in the gym, who kept encouraging you in your fitness plan, which wasn't easy at times, but now it's hard to keep you away from there.

It's not all about the 'me's in prison and the support you've been given here, but also the help from outside. Your probation officer who keeps referring you to agencies, even though you rarely turn up. And what about those at your local Drug Treatment Service and your GP, who keeps on working alongside you? They do this even when you appeared to have given up on yourself and might press the self-destruct button.

I'm sure members of your family could say, 'And what about me?' They may be out of touch now but once, way back, they had hopes that you would turn things around – they even paid for 'rehab'.

And there's still your nan and one friend who
still answers the phone to you when you call.

It's not all about you and me. There are so many others
who you've rubbed shoulders with, inside and out. Quite
a few duty governors have given you some time, listening
to you and trying to sort things out. Plus, there's the visits
staff who arranged that emergency visit from the sister
of your friend when he died. And that charity who looked
after your belongings when you were homeless, and
hopefully they still are.

So many people, those you know and those who have done
things for you that you don't even know about, especially
that charity, which made loads of phone calls, got
someone to pick up your stuff and then arranged storage
for it. And there are yet more people ready to support
you, like the women's charity and your aunt. Or maybe you
don't know about your aunt's involvement? Enough said!

As for me and the extended team, all we want is for you
to be at peace with yourself and the world around you,
to feel safe and know that your life is worth something.
What that looks like in practice is unique to you. However,
as your release gets closer, we believe there is more
you could achieve outside, yet we are mindful that it's
not what we believe that counts, but what you believe,
and we can't tell you what that is. It's up to you.

Chapter Three: The Butterfly

A week to go before your release and you're still 'cheesed off' at being let down at the planning meeting. 'Cheesed off' is polite. You are still very angry and you let everybody on the landing know it.

It's lunchtime lock-up and you take your food to your cell upstairs. You don't have to switch on the telly in your cell as you left it on all morning. You don't care about wasting electricity, in fact you don't care about much. It's a surprise you haven't got into trouble and had the telly taken away. You sit at the worktop, which is next to the bed, and after staring at the food you take a few bites: it's chicken . . . something. You suspect the chicken asked to be put down as it tastes like it was on its 'last legs' a long time ago.

It's noisy on the landing. Someone a couple of cells down has their radio on full blast and the girl next door is standing at the railings shouting to someone on the ground below. This is pretty normal for lunchtime – it can get really loud. Sometimes, even late at night, prisoners can still be making a noise in their cells, with the telly turned up high.

At other times, it can get very quiet. Especially in the middle of the night, but then you may hear someone nearby shedding a tear and their neighbour calling through the air-vent – 'You alright babes?' However, at lunchtime bang-up when the doors are locked it is normally quiet.

'Behind your doors,' is shouted by the officer and moments later, your door is shut and bolted. You stare at the telly in anticipation that shortly a prison officer is going to knock on your door and look through your window as part of the roll-count procedure, checking that the right number of prisoners are on the wing and in the prison. You don't want to give them the satisfaction of seeing your face but neither do you want to hide.

Prisoners have been known to hide, just because they want to mess up roll-count. Usually it's the younger ones, winding up the officers; they get mad if they have to count too many times and they can get in big trouble. It does their heads in as counting isn't one of their strong points. And if counting is delayed then unlock is delayed and everybody is angry. Roll-count appears to go smoothly this time.

After a while, things go quiet; it appears that today, they've got officers who can count. With no one likely to knock on your door, you decide it's safe to go to the toilet.

Back at your worktop, you sit on your green plastic chair, looking at the telly with your feet tipping you backwards on two legs. On the blue painted wall behind the telly are old toothpaste blobs. Toothpaste is used to stick things to the wall – photos and pictures. But you have no photos or pictures to put up. As you lean back on your chair, you notice there is a butterfly on your wall. It's high up, next to the open shelves where you keep your clothes.

Not that you have many to put there: a pair of leggings, a couple of plain T-shirts with some underwear tucked under them, your trainers and a pair of sliders are on the bottom shelf. You did have a nice coat when you came in, but it's gone now. You stare at the butterfly it's not doing anything, it's just there. But you're uncomfortable with it being in your six-by-ten-foot cell. The truth is you don't really like insects. If it was a spider, you would have tried to usher it out under the small gap at the bottom of your cell door. Your opening windows have been replaced with ones that don't move, fixed behind thick, square grey bars. The only air that comes into your room from outside comes through a grate, which is no good for scooping up insects and throwing them out alive. If there was a fly in the cell, you are more likely to swat it than wait for unlock.

And if you had a wasp in the cell – it's either you or the wasp – but one of you isn't going to survive. However, what you have on your wall is not a creepy crawly but a sizeable butterfly. Its wings are closed, displaying a mottled brown undercarriage. You don't want to kill it, but you don't want it there either. Often, after you've eaten lunch you lie on the bed and try to doze for half an hour, but with the butterfly in such close proximity, you know you can't relax.

During unlock you would normally ask an officer to help you get the butterfly out and some of the prisoners would probably assist. But in bang-up, things are different; only in an emergency are the cell doors opened. If there was a manic stinging wasp, you might get some sympathy from an intercom chat with an officer, possibly the only one on duty during the lunch period.

It's very unlikely they would open your door but rather tell you to ignore it. Yet you know if you reported that you were distressed because of a butterfly on your wall, you'd be laughed at, and for several days. If you maintain the importance of it being dealt with, the advice is more likely to be to kill it, like any other insect, with no mercy shown.

You retreat to your uncomfortable bed and prop yourself up with the one pillow you're allowed. Wedged in one corner, you look diagonally across the room, keeping a fixed gaze on the intruder. It's not moving but you don't think it's dead. Dead would be easy – scoop it up and flush it down the toilet. But it's horizontal on the wall and, sadly, you notice the occasional twitch of its wings. It's alive. This butterfly has ruined your lunch, your rest and your life – well, for now anyway. But somehow, you can't bring yourself to kill it.

Full of annoyance and frustration, your body is extremely tense. It's a hot day and now you're feeling even hotter. However, you start to think about the butterfly itself, rather than the pain it is causing you. It probably wasn't its choice to end up in your cell and would probably much prefer to be flying outside, free. Although, you think of all the risks it faces on the outside: predators, birds and frustrated humans. You're reminded that the lifespan of a butterfly is relatively short, from a day or two to a week or so, if it's lucky.

And its luck doesn't appear to be in. Even if you don't kill it, without nourishment it isn't going to survive long. You might as well kill it, put it out of its misery. Which brings you to think, 'Does it have misery?' You have misery but crediting an insect with that level of feeling is a bit farfetched. One moment it's here, then it's gone and who cares? You bet it doesn't even care. No one cares, so why should you? No one will even know it existed if you kill it and no one will miss it.

Angry, you stand up and stare at the butterfly, 'I bet you don't care if I kill you, do you?' you say out loud, but not loud enough for your neighbour to hear.

'Go on, kill me if you dare,' it answers back.

'But killing you would make a mess of the wall.'

'Who cares if there's a mess on the wall?
I don't,' you hear it reply.

So many thoughts. You are distracted by something
on the telly and sit back on the bed for a moment.
Then you look up again and it's still there. The slight
break enables another more friendly thought.

'It isn't your fault you're here,' you say, talking to the
butterfly. 'And if you didn't fly into my cell, then you could
have ended up in someone else's, and they may have killed
you by now, or you might have flown up to the roof, to
the skylight where the bright summer sunshine would
have burnt you alive.' You point past the door towards the
communal area above which has the skylight. 'Or you would
have fluttered to exhaustion and died. Do you really want to
die?' You stop a moment, shake your head and groan because
you know you're going soft and this isn't the normal 'you'.

For some reason, this change in attitude continues
and you wonder about rescuing the stranded butterfly.
Nobody needs to know what you're thinking and that you
want to save it, if that is what you really want to do. The
conversation in your head continues, 'I don't like butterflies.
I don't hate butterflies. Who cares about butterflies?'

Now you're annoyed with yourself for giving so much
thought to a flipping butterfly. Having spent so much
mental energy on it, you decide you're going to rescue
it, but how? You've seen people on the telly pick up
butterflies holding their wings together with their thumb
and index finger. But you don't want to get that close, and
anyway, what if you squashed its wings and broke them?

You look around your cell for something to help you catch
it. You decide on using one of your trainers. Taking out

the laces, you widen the trainer, pulling the tongue out as far as it will go. Then you take off the pillowcase, ready to carefully put the trainer inside it. You hope that the butterfly can rest in the shoe and not be squashed by the pillowcase, but still be stopped from flying around the cell.

You put an empty envelope on the top shelf, making sure you don't freak the butterfly. Armed with the trainer and with the pillowcase tucked into your baggy, grey, prison-issued jogging bottoms, you climb onto the toilet and carefully balance over the shelves.

'Now stay still,' you whisper to the butterfly, engaging it in conversation once more.

But this time, it doesn't reply. With two hands you slowly bring the trainer over the butterfly and hold it there. You use the envelope to slide under where you think the insect is and with one hand pressing the trainer on the wall, keeping the envelope in place, you grab the pillowcase and put it over the trainer and against the wall. Holding the pillowcase, trainer and the envelope, you pull all the components away from the wall at the same time. You look at the wall – no stain.

Presuming that the butterfly is in the trainer and the envelope is keeping it there, you wrap the pillowcase around both the shoe and the envelope. Now you hear a quiet fluttering noise. Carefully, you dismount the toilet and standing in the middle of your small single cell, you are suddenly aware you have no idea what you are going to do next.

Sitting on your bed, still holding everything, you start to think of the next steps. You wrap the pillowcase even tighter around the trainer and put it sole down on the worktop – at least it isn't going anywhere. Now to get some 'shut eye'. Moments later, there's a knock on your door and it opens. The officer shouts, 'Get yourselves ready for work.' That butterfly has done it again; it's ruined any chance of getting some rest, as you have spent all this time rescuing it.

For a split second, you think of throwing the trainer, pillowcase and butterfly on the floor and jumping on it. Then you think of the mess it would make of the trainer and you only have one pair of trainers. After a couple of minutes of unlock, you stand at your door with one trainer on and the other in the pillowcase.

Eventually, you attract the officer's attention, who shouts at you to put both your trainers on. You shout back, which isn't exactly helpful, but the officer comes over. Explaining the butterfly is in the shoe, inside the pillowcase, you suggest you are escorted to the yard where you can release the butterfly.

The officer agrees but locks you up behind your door for another twenty minutes before they get back to you. Together, you walk to the yard, one trainer on and one in your pillowcase. The SO (Supervising Officer), a senior officer, shouts at the officer for escorting you with only one shoe on. The officer signals that he'll explain later. You get outside and you go to a shrub and carefully remove the trainer from the pillowcase.

'P*** off and don't come back,' you say to the butterfly. You couldn't say 'go, fly, be happy' or anything nice, not with the officer around. He would have laughed at you and told everyone and you didn't want anyone knowing about this. But there's no sign of the butterfly. You look in the pillowcase and it isn't there. The officer is beginning to make uncomplimentary comments, when you notice it was further down the trainer than you anticipated.

But was it alive? You shake it and amazingly it doesn't only move but, after a few seconds, flies off. You watch it stop briefly on the shrubs, before it rises and is quickly out of sight. As it landed on the shrubs, it revealed its true colours; they were vibrant and beautiful, like a perfect piece of art. Its black upper wings had red stripes with white spots on the wing tips, its body had a blue glow about it, and you stood there, transfixed by its beauty.

It isn't long before the officer, feeling vindicated, makes you put on your other lace-less trainer and marches you – somewhat awkwardly – back to the wing before going to explain himself to the SO. Another officer is detailed to march you to the art workshop where you're working. You have no time to reflect – that will have to wait until later.

When you get back to the wing after work, one of the other inmates, who works on the wing, calls you over. With delight, she tells you she heard two of the other prisoners (who you don't get on with) laugh about putting a butterfly in your cell earlier, because they wanted to wind you up. Just then, everyone is called to get their evening meal. You go over to the two prisoners and confront them – with some annoyance.

They maintain their innocence and say they only ushered the butterfly into your room because they thought it was going to fly off and get stuck and they thought you would know what to do with it. Apparently, it was on the railings just outside your cell door. You don't know who or what to believe. You get your food and go to your room, somewhat irritated. A short while later, there's the shout to fill up your flasks and get ready for the night bang up.

Chapter Four: The Release

This time you get to eat the food and then wash up the plastic plate and cutlery in your small washbasin. It's the same basin you use for your daily strip wash and where you brush your teeth, when you get round to it. Sadly, your teeth aren't as good as you'd like them to be – years of neglect and drug use have prematurely decayed them. You are careful how you smile these days, usually with your mouth closed. The telly's still on, but you're not particularly interested. As you sit back on your bed, you look up to where the butterfly was and wonder – where is it now?

Is it still alive, did it find somewhere to feed, was it eaten by a bird or die of natural causes? Then you stop yourself and think – what do I care? But the truth is, you did care if only because it took so much time to rescue and you did a good job. All that effort was worth it. You knew you weren't going to get any thanks, but that's not why you did it. You did it because it was there, annoying you. You did it because you could, and that felt good. No one thanked you. The officer wasn't too happy, and their senior, even less so. In fact, you told the inmates you'd flushed it down the toilet. You have to keep them thinking you're 'hard'.

It appears that roll-count, once again, has been successfully completed and, once again, you ignore the officer. You watch telly from your bed and eventually drift off to sleep. In the middle of the night, you wake to hear the night officer clumsily shoving paperwork under your door. For a while, you ignore it. But eventually, unable to get back to sleep, you pick it up as you go to the loo. You get back into bed and see its writing paper, two empty envelopes and one sealed envelope. You open the sealed envelope and begin to read the note by the light of the telly, as the telly is still on with the sound down — you like the company.

> Yup, it's me again. I've written to you, explaining that there is another hastily arranged release-plan meeting. The outside probation team have requested a phone call 'meeting' with you and Housing have agreed again to turn up, Recovery have promised to send someone from their team, and they are hoping for one or two others to be there. The probation officer is stating how important it is for everyone to get behind you. The meeting is for 11:00 tomorrow morning in the group legal visits room.

> P.S. Well done for rescuing the butterfly.

Your first thoughts were, 'What? How does anyone outside of the house block know about the butterfly incident and why should they? You read the note again, but now you're beginning to get angry. How dare they arrange another meeting? They screwed up the first time — with no one coming, why should they demand another one? I was there. Where were they?' What a nerve, you think. 'If I screwed up and didn't attend a meeting, I'd be recalled to prison, but they just carry on as though nothing has happened.' You go on to highlight that there was no apology in the note.

'What a cheek!'

In anger and frustration, you screw up the note and aim for the toilet, but you miss. Still fuming, you pick up the note from the floor and read it again, your anger now bursting out with every thought. 'How dare they treat me like this? What am I, a piece of . . . dirt?' After a moment you decide not to dispose of the note but rather save it to show to your solicitor or show the governor. You put the crumpled note on the worktop and lie back on your bed, now wide awake, adrenalin pumping through your body.

Once again, you look up across the cell to where the butterfly was. Thinking about it, you whisper to yourself, 'You're lucky you're not still here, mate. You'd be down the loo if you were.' You know you could have taken your anger out on the defenceless insect. Breathing heavily, you put your hands behind your head to stop you from thumping the thin mattress either side of you. Scum, that's what they are, you think, still bubbling with rage.

Again, you look across the room and again you talk silently to the butterfly, which of course is no longer there. 'Bet you're glad you're out of this place.' Calming ever so slightly, you remember that shortly, you too will be out of this place. You smile when you also remember the film, *Shawshank Redemption*, when Red gets out of prison and meets up with Andy.

You imagine meeting up with the butterfly – 'We made it.' The image of the two of you together, comes to mind. 'We're not exactly normal main character material, are we?' You ponder further and break out into a huge grin. You and the butterfly taking on the world doesn't quite have the feel of a box office hit, but that doesn't bother you. You're both underdogs.

Underdogs need each other and the butterfly needed you today. You reflect on the moment you released the insect and on how you felt. It was a good feeling.

To be fair, it was probably the best feeling you'd had in days. You had made a difference and it felt real good.

'Probably feel better now than when I'm released myself,' you muse.

And now your thoughts turn back to your release in a few days' time. Suddenly, the lightness around you and image of meeting the butterfly on some remote beach is replaced with a darker, more sober feeling of sadness and anxiety. The feelings of no happy ending, no home, no one there for you and having to fight for yourself out on the street, drag you down again. This time it's not frustration but hopelessness that consumes you. 'If only someone would rescue my life like I rescued the butterfly.

'Someone to scoop up this stuck person and put some protection around them, even cover them up for a short while and then see them released.' No sooner had that thought come when another pops into your head. 'This isn't a movie; this is life, and it sucks. No happy ending, no one around to save this waste of space. I might as well be dead. Who would really care?' Again, the image of the butterfly comes to mind and how you carefully rescued it, deciding it was worth saving. You didn't kill it or leave it to its own instincts, which would have allowed it to fly higher until there was no escape.

'Huh, "flying high",' you ponder as that's how you normally deal with problems. You get as 'out of it' as you can. Your emotions go up and down like a rollercoaster.

Your mind wanders as you wonder what Recovery – the drug support team – are going to say at the meeting. You guess that Housing will once again say, 'Go to the council housing team and they may find you somewhere,' etc., etc. But why is the meeting in the group room for legal visits? Who from outside is going to be there? Probation will be on the phone and all the rest are insiders. It puzzles you for a while and you just hope they haven't dragged your nan to the 'party'.

'That flipping butterfly' – but you say something much stronger – comes into your head yet again and you reflect on how it was rescued without it doing anything. How you wish you could be picked up and rescued without doing anything. But then you remember – it must have moved when the envelope was slipped under it. If it hadn't moved, the envelope would have potentially broken its legs and wings. It had to move with your plan.

It had little choice and right now, you feel you have little choice but to either say 'sod off' to the professionals or cave into their plans. Do you give it a go, attend the meeting and see what they have to say? Or do you remain fixed in your belief, that it's all a waste of time and nothing is going to change for you? You lie flat on the bed and roll onto your side and try to get a little sleep.

It's 11:00 the next morning, and where are you?

You walk into the meeting room, only a couple of minutes late as it took a while to find an officer to bring you over. You're greeted by the caseworker and, looking around, you recognise most of the people. Your probation officer is on a video link, not over the phone; she puts her hand up to acknowledge you. There's someone from Recovery there but not the Housing person. Typical, you think. One other person is in the room, but you don't think you recognise them or maybe vaguely.

'You know everyone here, so we don't need to introduce ourselves,' the caseworker says as they

all smile at you. You look at the unknown person
and pull a face that says, 'Who are they?'

She smiles back. 'You may not remember me?'

You shake your head slowly, buying time to work
out how you would know her.

'I'm your cousin. We used to play together at Nan's.'

'What the . . . flipping heck are you doing here?'
You stop yourself from blurting out what
you are really thinking which is along the
lines of 'What the . . . are you doing meddling
in my business? Get your nose out, I don't
want you here and knowing all my stuff.'

'Mum told me about what's been happening
with you. She got it from Nan,' she replies,
completely unfazed by your response.

'But why?' you say, shaking your head, whilst wearing a
blank look on your face – suggesting you don't care.

'We heard you needed a bed. The youngest
has left home and we thought we better fill it
before he comes back. Do you want it?'

You don't want to answer straight
away, so you ask, 'How's Nan?'

'She's OK but more to the point, how's you
and do you want this room or not?'

She's a bit pushy, you think to yourself. You look
at her; she could see you were thinking about this,

then she added, 'Well?' She raises her eyebrows.

'I don't need to be rescued,' you say bluntly.

'We're not rescuing you; we're offering you a bed.
Do you want it?' was her quick reply.

The truth was that you needed to be rescued but would never admit it. You nodded, she smiled, and you looked around at the people in the room and thought, what's just happened? Everyone was thinking the same. She looked straight at you and said, 'That's sorted then.'

But of course, it wasn't we had another hour to discuss issues and what was going to happen next. We even discussed you rescuing the butterfly – it had been recorded on your notes by the officer as the reason why you were late to work that afternoon. At least you understood why people knew about it and why Housing hadn't attended – they hoped they didn't need to.

It turned out that your cousin had been inside herself many years ago. She'd been in for a few weeks; something to do with non-payment of fines, failure to comply with a court order, not turning up for community service and contempt of court, and then failing to turn up again. Nan didn't know nor your mum. Eventually the fines were paid and things got sorted. Having had that experience, your cousin had a little insight into some of the issues you had been facing.

She found out from Nan where you were and decided to write to the prison, who then contacted your probation officer, who got back in touch with her. The first meeting didn't happen because your cousin couldn't make it. She and her partner decided they could make an offer of accommodation and wanted to do it in person, but she wasn't going to mess around. That was clear.

It was lunchtime when you got back. You collected your food, went to your cell, made a drink and then it was bang-up. Your head was spinning as you sat on the bed with your drink, looking up at the butterfly spot.

'Did you do this?' you said out loud, as though talking to the butterfly. Smiling to yourself you thought, 'One good turn deserves another, so now we're equal.' You even gave yourself a little chuckle. After a while, you reflected on how many people were at the meeting supporting you – four: Probation, Caseworker, Recovery and your cousin. Four people attended and four people had rescued the butterfly – the two inmates who ushered the butterfly into your cell, you and then the wing officer. How weird was that? You finished your drink and slept all through lock-up. It had been a crazy twenty-four hours.

A few days later, you walked out the huge wooden gate. The sun was still shining and you were wearing your sliders, jogging bottoms and T-shirt while carrying one small black holdall with only your paperwork in it. The paperwork was your licence which told you what your release conditions were. Things like which probation office you must report to and that you were to live only where your Community Offender Manager – Probation– says you can.

There was one other prisoner being released that morning. You didn't know her, and her English wasn't very good, but you could make out that her boyfriend was outside waiting for her. She didn't really want to chat and neither did you. When the gate rolled back, the other woman ran to her boyfriend and was promptly embraced into his arms. Usually, you had to walk past such scenes knowing there was no one waiting for you.

But not this time, because as agreed, your cousin was there, having driven for well over an hour in heavy traffic. I was also outside as I wanted to see your cousin and wave you off. After saying our 'goodbyes' you walked off to the car. There was a surprise waiting for you. In the back was your nan.

As soon as you saw her, you ran to the car, opened the rear door and jumped in alongside her. As she raised her frail arms to embrace you, you gave her the gentlest of 'little-bear hugs', wrapping your arms right around her. She slipped a 'fiver' into your pocket and gave you a wink. You gave her a kiss on the cheek and said, 'Love you, Nan.'

Part Two: Reflection

Chapter Five: Where are they now?

As I sit at the same table where I wrote this story, summer is on the cusp of turning to autumn and I'm thinking about writing again. Looking out the window I spot a butterfly, maybe for the last time this year. From where I sit, it looks brown, not like the many white ones I'd seen throughout the summer in my small garden. It's fluttering around a bush.

I am understandably reminded of the story and begin to reflect upon it. I start with an obvious question – Where are they now; You, Me and the Butterfly? Was the last page the end of the story or should it continue somewhere else? It could be very easy to continue the story.

You hit it off straight away with your cousin and made a few plans for the things you wanted to do together. You settle into the household routine in a way you never dreamt you would. You even managed to get a voluntary job at a local charity shop two mornings a week.

Or maybe, as soon as you drive away from prison, you began to argue with your cousin as she set out some ground rules for living in her place. You had hoped you had got away from being told when and what to do. That's it. Something snaps inside and you could decide you can't stay with her under that pressure.

As you near the house, you ask to be dropped off at the local shop where you're going to buy some cigarettes. You state somewhat bluntly that you will make your way to the house. You kiss Nan, hop out and are never seen again. A few weeks later, there's news that, sadly, you overdosed on a 'bad batch' and died.

Or? There are several different possibilities for the ending. Is what happened to You, Me and the Butterfly even known? Perhaps it is easier to speculate about the Butterfly as it's likely to be flying high in some other realm by now. Life, for some, moves on, as it did for You and Me.

You

There are several potential outcomes for You. These range from a 'happy ever after' ending, to one that took You back to prison. In many ways, it is the choice of the reader to decide for themselves what happened next. Some may choose to imagine a middle ground of staying out of prison but still struggling with addiction. Others, of course, would like to think that You managed to engage with valuable support services, which enabled You to manage or even breakthrough the cycle of dependency and criminality.

A lovely thought would be that You stayed at the cousin's house for several months, before moving into a private rental funded by housing benefit, but how realistic is that? And how realistic is it, to hope that being reconnected with Nan inspired You to see her weekly, speak to her daily and use this connection as motivation to address the issues and challenges You had faced in the past?

However, this may not mean everything was resolved – issues with close family and friends may still be there and health conditions may still arise as a result of those past addictions. Issues for You continue long after You leaves prison.

Me

The narrator for the story was the caseworker. They were in an ideal position to relay the events, as they talked to various people and had access to internal records and reports. Your caseworker highlighted how there were many other people involved in supporting You – many other 'Me's – workers of one description or another, as well as family.

Working in prison can be a challenging environment and many find, not long after they've started, that it's not for them. Others stick around for a while until a career move or a different job becomes tempting. Others appear to stick around forever, almost as though they're stuck or biding their time until they know what they want to do.

Or maybe they're waiting to save up enough money, or they're hit with unforeseen circumstances like illness and bereavement and it forces them to decide what or where their future lies. I'd like to think the narrator is still working in the prison and still wants to make a difference, but they, too, may have moved onto new challenges.

Us

Some readers of this story will have first-hand experience of prison life, but many won't. Prison is somewhere most of us can't imagine visiting, let alone living in for a few months. Sadly, for some people, prison is safer than being outside in the community. It is free from some of the abuse and temptations they encounter every day when 'on the out'. Inside, some prisoners learn new skills and get the medical treatment they have needed for a long time but never got around to it. They then reconnect with their family and community and, once released, never return. However, for some, prison is their worst nightmare. Thoughts of self-harm or worse come to mind. Some of us know what it's like to face desperate times, to feel imprisoned by hopelessness when we feel isolated, misunderstood, rejected, useless, worthless, side-lined and forgotten. We can have these feelings even if we appear to be successful or not. Whether we speak with confidence or shy away from conversation. However we appear to others, we may still have messed up and given up. The question is, will we give 'life' and those around us another chance?

Are we ready to be helped back to a position where we can 'fly' and let our 'true' and amazing colours be displayed?

Does reality allow for this when the last page is written?

Do we have people around who can journey with us?

Maybe there comes a time when we need to accept the help on offer. We need to be rescued, even though it's hard and hasn't worked out before. Perhaps someone close to us is stuck and needs our support to move on, to fly again. Can we help the 'butterfly' fly? Can there be a happy ending or a positive point reached on the journey? End results are important but so is the journey. And we're all on a journey. Sometimes, we just need to be rescued, held, released and ready to carry on.

It's worth reflecting that when a butterfly is resting or stuck, its underwings are on show, and these can often be less attractive than its iridescent upper wings which show their beautiful colours. It isn't until the butterfly flies away that its beauty can be seen. Sometimes, we may need to move for our more positive side to be seen. Making that first 'step', whether it be physical or emotional and mental, can be significant.

Conclusion

As you read this, you may have identified with one of the characters: You, Me or the Butterfly. Perhaps you can identify with two or even all three. Many of us have been close to giving up, unable to move on or to rise above our circumstances, just like 'You' in the story. Maybe some of us, having experienced what it is like to be stuck and struggling, are now in a position like 'Me' and able to offer support.

I'm guessing many of us can identify with the 'Butterfly' – stuck, trapped, not even knowing how we got there. All three can interact with each other; they just have to be willing. Even the butterfly needed to fly off to pastures new to fulfil its purpose.

Can you hope for an interaction or intervention that may transform your life? Will you accept it?

Or are you ready to support someone to engage and fly again?

Epilogue: A Letter

To You,

I've just seen a butterfly on a book cover – an image not a real one – and it has reminded me of the story. Sometimes things appear stuck like the butterfly or even out of our control. Challenges arise that we weren't expecting, or we're not equipped to deal with. Life can seem chaotic or confusing. Sometimes it's hard to keep some dreams alive or even expect nice things to happen.

But why shouldn't we hope for better or best? When I'm low, I have to remind myself that I am as valuable as the butterfly or as the person standing next to me. Right now, I'm facing some issues and asking myself some questions. If you're in the same position, they might be helpful for you too.

1. Am I ready to go again?

2. Can I do it on my own?

3. Do I need support, help or even rescuing?

4. How am I really feeling right now?

5. Do I have someone I can talk to, who is ready to help, and do I know how to contact them?

6. What practical help do I need?

7. What does 'hope' look like for me?

8. Can I share 'hope' with others?

Whenever you're feeling low and spot a butterfly, remember the story, and get ready to respond to the opportunities around you and never give up hoping.

Best wishes,

Me.

Acknowledgements

I would like to thank Malcolm Down Publishers – especially Malcolm, Sarah and Lydia for their input and support. Thanks also go to Samantha and Terry who read the initial manuscript and encouraged me to develop it.

I'm so grateful to my wife, my family and many friends who have supported me during this project.

A huge thank you goes to the women who have shared their stories with me as they have left the prison, I'm incredibly grateful to you all.